W9-BYF-899

STAR WARS®
A NEW HOPE

Adapted by Geof Smith
Illustrated by Caleb Meurer and Micky Rose

 A GOLDEN BOOK • NEW YORK

© & ™ 2017 LUCASFILM LTD. All rights reserved. Published in the United States by Golden Books, an imprint of Random House Children's Books, a division of Penguin Random House LLC, 1745 Broadway, New York, NY 10019, and in Canada by Penguin Random House Canada Limited, Toronto. Golden Books, A Golden Book, A Big Golden Book, the G colophon, and the distinctive gold spine are registered trademarks of Penguin Random House LLC.
randomhousekids.com
ISBN 978-0-7364-3692-2
Printed in the United States of America
10 9 8 7 6 5 4 3 2 1

A long time ago in a galaxy far, far away . . .

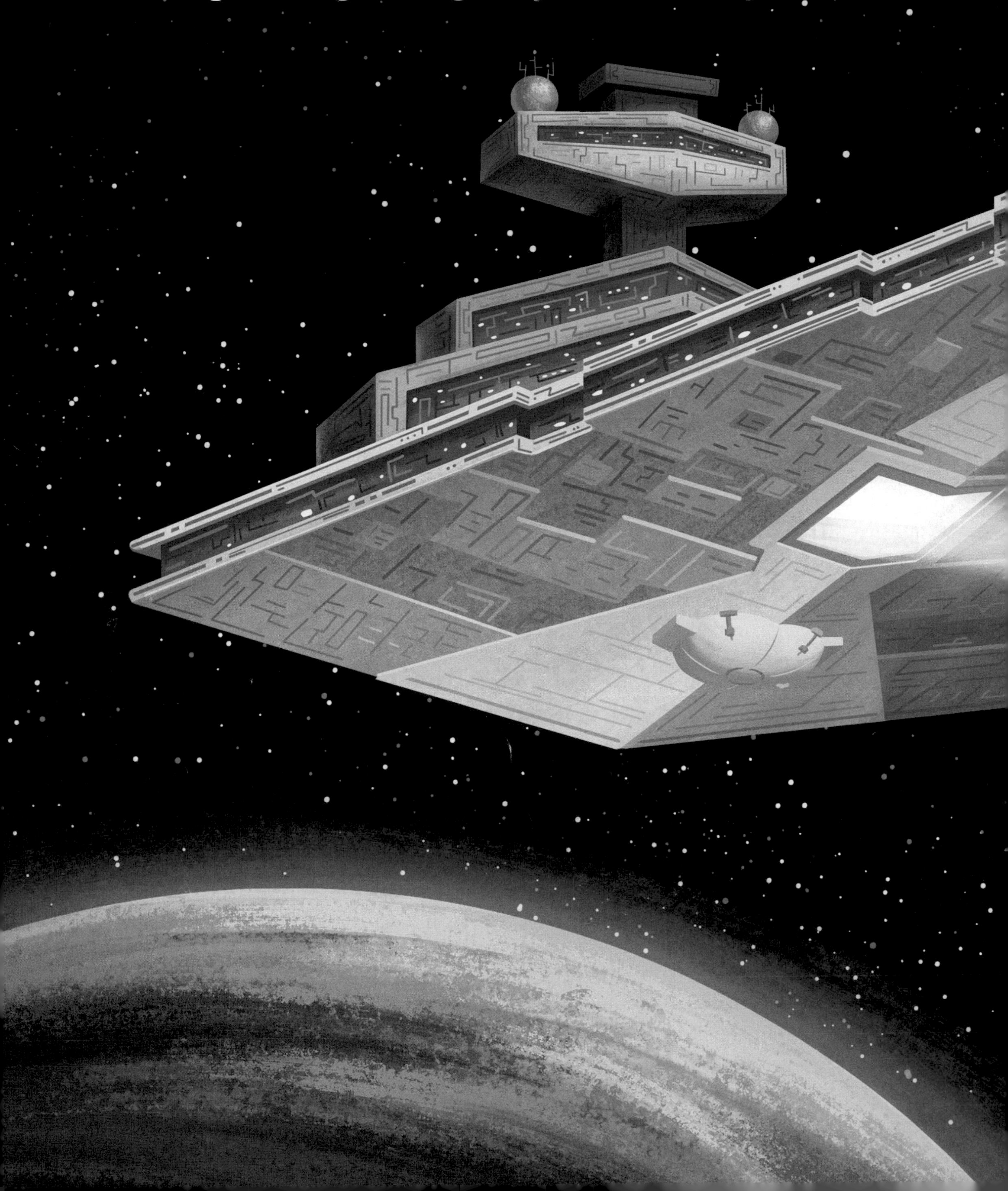

A terrible war raged as the **Rebel Alliance** struggled to defeat the evil Galactic Empire. Led by brave Princess Leia, a small team of rebels had just stolen secret plans for the Empire's ultimate weapon—the Death Star, a space station so powerful it could vaporize planets! But as the rebels tried to escape, an Imperial Star Destroyer captured them.

Princess Leia hid the plans and a secret message in a small droid named **R2-D2**. As R2-D2 and his friend **C-3PO** fled in an escape pod, a menacing figure cloaked in black invaded the rebel ship. It was the evil Imperial commander, **Darth Vader**!

The Imperial stormtroopers captured Princess Leia. Darth Vader **demanded** to know the location of the plans, but Leia pretended she knew nothing about them. As the princess was led away, she hoped little R2-D2 could complete his mission before Darth Vader caught on to her trickery.

Meanwhile, R2-D2 and C-3PO's pod landed on the desert
planet of Tatooine. After wandering the sandy dunes, the two
droids were **captured** by small scavengers called Jawas.

The droids were loaded onto the Jawas' giant sandcrawler. It was filled with other lost robots and abandoned machines. **"We're doomed,"** C-3PO said. "Do you think they'll melt us down?"

After a short trip, R2-D2 and C-3PO were unloaded and put up for sale. A farmer and his nephew, **Luke Skywalker**, bought them.

Luke dreamed of leaving his desert home and traveling into space for exciting adventures.

As Luke cleaned R2-D2, he accidentally unlocked part of Princess Leia's message. "Help me, **Obi-Wan Kenobi**. You're my only hope."

Luke wondered if she meant the old hermit Ben Kenobi, who lived far off in the desert.

That night, R2-D2 secretly rolled away to find Obi-Wan and deliver the message.

At dawn, Luke and C-3PO raced off in a landspeeder to find R2-D2. When they finally reached the little droid, they saw dangerous Tusken Raiders, also known as **Sand People**, in the distance.

Suddenly, the Sand People **attacked**!
Luckily, a mysterious cloaked figure came
to the rescue.

It was Ben Kenobi!

In Ben's hut, R2-D2 played Princess Leia's full message. The princess asked Obi-Wan to take the Death Star plans to her home planet of Alderaan. Luke was amazed to learn that old Ben was once Obi-Wan Kenobi, a great **Jedi Knight** skilled in the ways of the **Force**.

"The Force is an energy field that gives the Jedi Knight his power," Obi-Wan explained. "It binds the galaxy together."

Obi-Wan then revealed that Luke's father was also a Jedi Knight—until Darth Vader destroyed him. Vader had been a student of Obi-Wan's, but he turned to the **dark side of the Force**.

Obi-Wan gave Luke a gift—Luke's father's **lightsaber**, a powerful laser sword.

"I want to learn the ways of the Force and become a Jedi like my father," Luke said.

Luke and Obi-Wan sped to the Mos Eisley spaceport to find a pilot who could take them to Alderaan. But on the way, they were stopped by stormtroopers. Ben used a **Jedi mind trick** to confuse the troopers.

"These are not the droids you are looking for," Ben said with a wave of his hand.

"These are not the droids we are looking for," one trooper repeated.

Luke couldn't believe it!

Luke, Obi-Wan, and the droids reached the spaceport
and visited a cantina crowded with strange aliens.

Obi-Wan hired **Han Solo** and his Wookiee copilot, **Chewbacca**. Their ship, the *Millennium Falcon,* was fast enough to outrun Imperial Star Destroyers. It would be a dangerous trip, but Han needed the money to pay a debt he owed to **Jabba the Hutt**, a powerful gangster.

As Luke and his friends were boarding the *Millennium Falcon*, stormtroopers spotted them. **"Chewie, get us out of here!"** Han yelled as lasers sizzled past him.

The *Millennium Falcon* blasted off. Imperial Star Destroyers chased them, but Han quickly engaged the ship's hyperdrive. Soon the *Falcon* was traveling at the speed of light.

During the spaceflight, Chewbacca and R2-D2 played a game on a hologram table. When the little droid won a move, the big Wookiee **growled**.

C-3PO suggested a new strategy. "Let the Wookiee win!"

Obi-Wan began to train Luke to use his lightsaber.
The young man wore a helmet with the blast shield
down so he couldn't see.

"Stretch out with your feelings," Obi-Wan instructed.
Zap! Zap! Luke blocked two laser blasts from a
floating remote. The old Jedi was proud of his student.

The heroes raced across the galaxy, only to discover that Alderaan was gone! All that was left was a small moon.

"That's no moon," Obi-Wan said. It was the **Death Star**! The Empire had used the superweapon to destroy Princess Leia's home planet!

Suddenly, the giant space station pulled the *Falcon* in with a powerful **tractor beam**. The smaller ship landed inside the Death Star, and stormtroopers raced aboard to search for the heroes. But they couldn't find anyone.

Luke and his friends were hiding in the *Falcon*'s secret compartments. After they finally emerged, they snuck into the Death Star.

Obi-Wan immediately set off to deactivate the tractor beam so they could escape. As the others waited behind, R2-D2 made a discovery: Princess Leia was being held **prisoner** in the Death Star!

Disguised as stormtroopers, Luke and Han handcuffed Chewbacca and pretended he was a prisoner. They entered the detention center and took the guards by surprise.

Luke quickly found Princess Leia and opened her cell.

"I'm here to rescue you!"

Luke said, taking off his helmet.

The stormtroopers cornered Luke and his friends in the detention center.

"You came in here, but didn't you have a plan for getting out?" Princess Leia asked.

Thinking fast, she grabbed a blaster and blew
open a **garbage chute**. The heroes dove in.

Luke, Princess Leia, Han, and Chewbacca landed in a giant trash compactor filled with stinky junk.

"What an incredible smell you've discovered," Han said to the princess.

Suddenly, the walls began to close in, getting **closer** and **closer** and **closer**! The friends were trapped. Things looked grim.

Luke used his comlink to contact C-3PO and R2-D2.

At the last second, the droids were able to turn off the compactor and unlock the door. Luke and his friends crawled out of the muck to safety.

Meanwhile, Obi-Wan found the power for the tractor beam and turned it off. It was time to escape—if everyone could reach the *Falcon*.

As Luke and his friends raced back to their ship, stormtroopers chased them. In the confusion, Luke and Leia were separated from Han and Chewbacca. They ran right to the edge of a **deep chasm**.

"I think we took a wrong turn," Luke said.

Luke quickly unwound a grappling hook and cable from his belt and threw it. He and Leia were able to **swing** across the chasm before the stormtroopers could catch them!

Obi-Wan confronted his old enemy
Darth Vader. They ignited their
lightsabers—and the duel began!

As Luke ran to the *Millennium Falcon,* he saw the battle—
just as Vader struck Obi-Wan! But the old man simply
vanished. His cloak fell to the floor as the Jedi became one
with the Force.
"Nooo!" cried Luke.

The heroes raced aboard the *Millennium Falcon* and took off.

Imperial TIE fighters tried to shoot them down. But Han and Luke climbed into the *Falcon*'s gunner seats and **blasted** them to bits! Soon the friends were zooming across the galaxy to deliver the secret Death Star plans to the rebels.

At their base, the rebels reviewed the Death Star plans and found a weakness. One perfect shot in a small exhaust port could destroy the entire station!

But the rebels needed to act fast—the Death Star was preparing to **wipe out** the rebel base!

Han told Luke that he didn't want to help with the mission. Instead, the pilot was returning to Tatooine to pay his debt to Jabba the Hutt.

Luke hopped in an X-wing fighter with R2-D2 and joined the rebel pilots in their attack on the Death Star. Waves of screaming TIE fighters defended the station.

Luke flew his X-wing down a narrow trench toward the vent.

Suddenly, Darth Vader appeared in a TIE fighter!

Darth Vader was about to destroy Luke's X-wing when a blast rocked his TIE fighter. It was the *Millennium Falcon*, **zooming to the rescue**!

"You're all clear, kid!" shouted Han. "Now let's blow this thing and go home!"

As Darth Vader's damaged fighter spiraled into space,
Luke heard Obi-Wan's voice: **"Use the Force."**

Luke turned off his targeting
computer, closed his eyes, and fired.
The shot was perfect.

The Death Star **exploded**!

Luke Skywalker and his friends were **heroes**! Princess Leia gave them medals, and the rebels cheered.

Their fight with Darth Vader and the Empire was far from over. But thanks to Luke, Leia, and Han, the rebels had a new hope.